North American
Ocean Creatures

By Colleayn O. Mastin ✹ Illustrated by Jan Sovak

Grasshopper
BOOKS PUBLISHING

Cod

Millions of codfish used to swim
Off the North Atlantic shore,
But something sad has happened,
And these millions swim no more.

Some say it was overfishing
That made cod stocks so low;
While others think it was hungry seals
That caused the cod to go.

The number of cod found in the Atlantic Ocean became so low that the cod fishery in the maritime provinces had to be shut down. Hopefully, the codfish will return if fishing is stopped for a few seasons.

Each female codfish can lay millions of eggs each year. These eggs float freely in the ocean until they hatch into little fish.

Young codfish feed on plankton, which consists of small plants and animals that float in the sea. When the cod are older, they live by eating other fish.

Cod are big eaters, and the more they eat the bigger they grow. (People stop growing at a certain age, but many fish keep growing as long as they live.)

Goosefish

On the top of a goosefish's ugly head,
There's a kind of "fishing line,"
With a "worm" on the end to lure other fish
On which this big eater can dine.

As soon as an unlucky fish swims by,
The goosefish opens its jaws,
Then into its mouth the fish is sucked,
To be swallowed without a pause.

Goosefish lie on the bottom of the ocean floor waiting for anything edible to come near. They are greedy eaters, and their huge mouths can swallow fish nearly as large as themselves.

They have been known to capture ducks and geese that were diving into deep water looking for something to eat.

The goosefish has a huge mouth lined with needle-sharp teeth. When this mouth is snapped open suddenly, it creates a suction that sends the victim down into the goosefish's stomach.

Goosefish can grow to be over one meter (three feet) long. Because of the way they catch other fish, they belong to a group of fish known as anglers. (An angler is a person who enjoys fishing.)

Octopus

An "octo-puss" is something like
A wet, eight-legged cat.
If one should jump upon your lap,
What would you think of that?

The biggest type of octopus
Is dangerous, we are told,
But the little ones will run away,
For they sure aren't very bold.

Octopuses have large, slit eyes. They roam the ocean floor looking for food. When they find something they would like to eat, such as a crab, they pounce on it like a cat. Then they grab their victim in their sucker-bearing arms and break open its shell with their strong mouths and sharp, parrotlike beaks.

Octopuses are not fish. They belong to a group of creatures called mollusks. Some mollusks—such as clams, mussels, oysters and snails—have a soft body inside a hard shell. Others like the octopus and the slug have a soft body, but no shell.

The octopus has many enemies, and to escape it shoots a stream of dark inklike fluid into the water. This ink acts as a screen giving the octopus time to flee from an attacker. It can also escape by stretching out so thin that it can easily slide through a crack in rocks under the sea.

Two of the largest octopuses in the world are found off the shores of North America, one in the Atlantic Ocean and one in the Pacific. The giant Pacific octopus can stretch at least seven meters, (twenty-three feet) from arm to arm.

Dogfish

A dogfish is a smallish shark,
With spines you shouldn't touch;
They're very speedy swimmers,
But no one likes them much.

Those who fish just hate them,
And wish they'd go away
But dogfish are survivors,
And it seems they're here to stay.

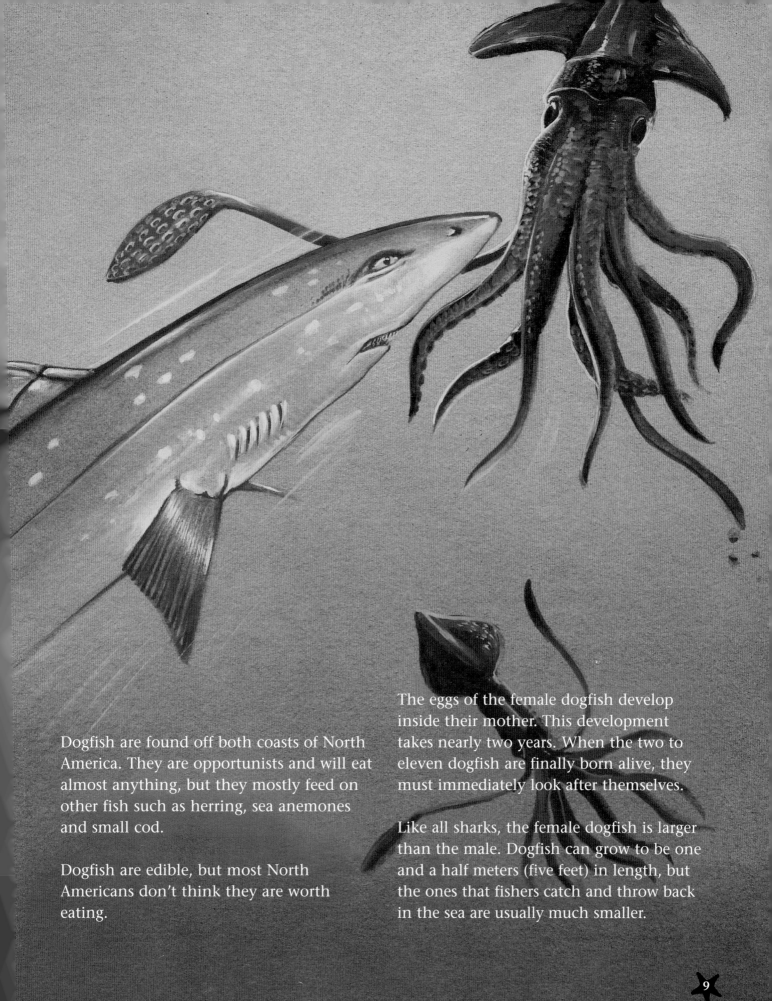

Dogfish are found off both coasts of North America. They are opportunists and will eat almost anything, but they mostly feed on other fish such as herring, sea anemones and small cod.

Dogfish are edible, but most North Americans don't think they are worth eating.

The eggs of the female dogfish develop inside their mother. This development takes nearly two years. When the two to eleven dogfish are finally born alive, they must immediately look after themselves.

Like all sharks, the female dogfish is larger than the male. Dogfish can grow to be one and a half meters (five feet) in length, but the ones that fishers catch and throw back in the sea are usually much smaller.

Clam

A clam lives near the ocean,
In a hole on a sandy beach,
Where it tries to keep out of
A clam-digger's reach.

This clam's life would be longer
And its laugh would be louder,
If we didn't dig them up
To make clam chowder.

Clams must be very careful and quick not to end up as dinner for one of their many enemies. When they sense danger, they must do a very fast disappearing act. The faster and deeper they dig, the safer they are.

Clams are an important food source for fish, birds and humans.

The shells of clams are entirely protective in nature. The clam gathers food by drawing a current of water inside its shell with its siphon. Then it filters the food particles from the water with its gills.

Clams lay eggs that are left in the ocean to survive on their own. Some parents protect the eggs until they are developed enough to survive their enemies.

Giant clams, which live in the Indian and Pacific oceans grow almost a meter (three feet) wide, and can weigh up to one hundred and thirty kilograms (286 pounds).

Sea Horse

A very odd fish is the sea horse;
It really is quite strange,
Looking something like a cowboy,
Might ride out on the range.

Sea horses swim rather slowly,
On their heads is a long skinny snout,
Which they use to suck up their dinner
Made of anything swimming about.

Sea horses are probably the only fish in the ocean that swim in a stately, upright position. They can rest from swimming by holding on to a piece of seaweed with their monkey-like tails.

An especially odd thing about sea horses is that the female of the species places her eggs in the kangaroolike brood pouch of the male. He carries the eggs around for about two weeks until they turn into little sea horses that swim away on their own.

Pipefish, which are cousins to the sea horse, also share the same strange "Mr. Mom" style of reproduction.

Sea horses come in several colors—red, brown, yellow and green—but can change their color to match their surroundings. This protects them from their enemies and makes them hard to see when they are searching for food.

Salmon

The salmon of the West Coast
All have a silvery look;
Their names are chum and coho,
Sockeye, pink and chinook.

Salmon are born in a river,
But spend their life at sea;
Then they return to the river they came from—
How they find it is a mystery.

The return home of the sockeye salmon is especially dramatic. After spending four years in the ocean, they head up a river to find the stream where they were born.

When they enter freshwater, they undergo a startling change in color. From silver, they turn bright red along the sides and green on the head.

After reaching their home stream, the salmon dig a nest, lay their eggs and cover them with gravel. Then they die. The eggs hatch in the winter, and soon after, the young "smolt" head back to the ocean to begin the cycle again.

Some ichthyologists (people who study fish) now think that salmon are guided back to their home river or stream by their strong sense of smell.

Electric Ray

An electric ray is a strange fish
That could give you a terrible shock;
An electric ray could do just that:
It would feel like a smack with a rock.

These shocking fish don't swim around,
But just lie there covered in sand;
If by chance you stepped on one,
You'd wish you had stayed on land.

One jolt from an electric ray could knock you right off your feet. An electric ray can produce a charge of electricity twice as strong as the current that comes from an electric plug in your home.

As they lie on the bottom of the ocean, these lazy and slow swimmers feed on worms, shrimp and other small fish. Usually, they will catch their dinner by stunning it with an electric shock.

The largest electric rays are about two meters (six feet) long, but most are much smaller.

The young electric rays are hatched from eggs held inside the body of their mother.

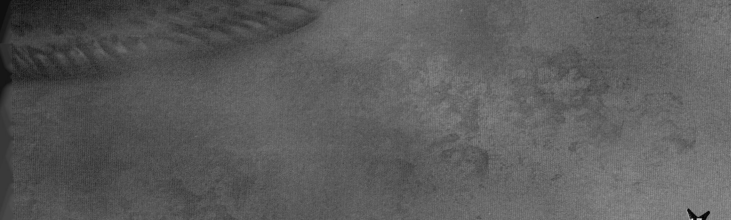

Great White Shark

*The most scary thing in the ocean
Is this shark that's huge and white;
There's nothing that it meets with
That it's afraid to fight.*

*The tall black fin on the great white's back
Cuts the surface like a knife;
If you ever see this man-eater's fin,
Swim to shore to save your life.*

The great white shark is among the most savage of hunters in the ocean. It feeds on sea otters, sea lions, fish, seals and crabs. It will even attack that other dangerous ocean-dweller, the killer whale.

The great white shark is clearly the most dangerous shark and has attacked humans on both the Atlantic and Pacific coasts.

A great white shark is ovoviviparous, which means that the mother hatches her eggs within her body, so the young are born alive. When they are born, the young are about one to two meters (three to six feet) in length. They immediately begin their hunt for food.

One group of fish—such as salmon, sardine and trout—have a skeleton made of bones. Another group, which includes sharks and rays, have a skeleton made of cartilage.

Dolphin

A dolphin is a kind of whale,
Although it's much, much smaller;
These dolphins make a lot of noise:
And like to bark and holler.

Far out in the rolling ocean
Great herds of dolphins play;
They swim, and leap and dive a lot,
And chase their food all day

Dolphins really seem to get great joy out of being alive. Sometimes they will be seen riding along the bow waves of a ship. They balance on the waves and get a free ride as the ship moves along.

In a herd of dolphins there may be as many as a thousand individuals. The herd doesn't swim about aimlessly, but follows the fish and squid that they feed on. Female dolphins give birth to their young. The young are looked after until they are old enough to survive on their own.

Dolphins main enemies are whales and man. Sometimes many dolphins get caught in fishing nets.

A fully grown dolphin is about three meters (ten feet) long. A dolphin can enjoy its life in the ocean for as long as thirty years. However, a dolphin placed in captivity is likely to die of a broken heart. Dolphins like to be free.

21

Sea Anemone

Anemones look like a flower,
But they're an animal, not a plant,
For anemones can move about,
And a tree or flower can't.

Anemones must also catch their food,
Which plants don't have to do;
They reach out an "arm" to catch a fish,
Which is strange, but also true.

The arm the anemone uses to catch food is called a tentacle. Each anemone has many tentacles, all of which are armed with stinging cells.

When an unfortunate small animal, such as a shrimp or a fish, touches these cells it is paralyzed and then pulled into the anemone's stomach.

Although an anemone is usually fixed by its base to a rock, it can free itself and tumble through the water to another location. Sometimes it will do this to escape from a predator such as a sea slug.

Anemones in many beautiful colors are found in all the oceans of the world. The largest are about a meter (three feet) across. The smallest is the size of a pinhead.

Orca (or Killer Whale)

When killer whales go hunting,
They do so in a pack;
This doesn't give much chance to
The creatures they attack.

Killer whales make lots of sounds,
Their swimming is not slow;
Their colors are most striking,
Slick black and white below.

Killer whales are the largest of the dolphin family. These big, intelligent animals are excellent and cunning hunters. They are sometimes called "sea wolves."

Like wolves killer whales hunt in packs. They prey on other whales, otters, seals, sharks, penguins, seabirds and fish. When they go hunting together, orcas seem to be able to "talk" to each other. This helps them work together as a team.

Young orcas are born in the winter and are looked after by both parents. At birth an orca is about two meters (six feet) long.

They do not appear to be afraid of sharks and are quite unafraid of approaching ships.

Hagfish

It's hard to love a hagfish,
Those sort of eel-like creatures,
With such unpleasant habits
And unattractive features.

The way a hagfish feeds itself
Isn't pleasant to think about—
It creeps inside an edible fish,
And eats its insides out.

The hagfish has a series of slime pores lining its belly. This slime is used as a defense against it enemies and as a way to scare other fish away.

This slime is such an effective defense system that the hagfish must tie itself in a knot and then slip through it to get the slime away from itself. If it didn't it could die from lack of oxygen.

This eel-like creature needs six hearts to pump blood through its long body. It has one main heart, two in its head, two in its tail and one in its liver. It lives in the mud at the bottom of the sea. Its eyes are not visible.

The hagfish feeds on dead or dying fish or those caught in a net. It enters the body cavity of its victim and devours the soft inner tissues. Another strange feature of this fish is that its mouth is toothless, but it has teeth on its tongue!

The hagfish is not popular with fishers because often they recover their catch only to find a bag of fish skin, bones and hagfish.

Sturgeon

Sturgeons are a rare fish,
Their skins like armor plate,
With their long snouts, they dig up food,
That helps them put on weight.

They swim in lakes or oceans,
But no matter where they are,
They give us lots of tasty meat,
And salty caviar.

The salty eggs of sturgeon are called caviar and are considered a delicacy to eat. However, because sturgeon have long been prized for their tasty meat and eggs, too many of them have been caught. The white sturgeon is now on the endangered species list.

The sturgeon is among the most ancient of fishes. It has been swimming in the world's lakes, rivers and oceans for at least sixty-five million years.

A sturgeon can live for one hundred and fifty years. Lake sturgeon do not grow as big as those that live in the ocean.

The sturgeon is a bottom feeder. Like the codfish, it has whiskers called barbels hanging from its mouth. These help it find worms and shellfish buried in the mud where this strange fish finds food.

Flying Fish

A flying fish can't really fly,
But can leap out of the ocean,
And skim across the surface
With a sort of flying motion.

These awesome fish travel in large schools,
And it's truly a wonderful sight,
When several leave the water,
For a short and speedy flight.

It is thought that the reason flying fish leave the water is to escape from bigger fish such as tuna or mackerel.

By beating its tail rapidly on the surface of the ocean, a flying fish can leap into the air. Then it expands its large winglike fins and soars over the ocean.

Because a flying fish cannot flap its fins the way a bird flaps its wings, it cannot stay airborne for very long. But through a series of short flights, it can cover a distance of around four hundred meters (1300 feet) before dropping back into the ocean.

Flying fish eggs are covered with long silky threads that attach to kelp or other floating objects, keeping them safe while they await hatching.

Published by
Grasshopper Books Publishing
106 Waddington Drive
Kamloops, British Columbia
Canada V2E 1M2

This book is dedicated to my favorite oldest daughter Kelly Ann and to Dave Meston

Acknowledgments:
The author wishes to thank the following for their help and contributions to this book: Emelee Marchant, Graham Gillespie, Government of Canada, Ocean Research, Naniamo, British Columbia, Dennis Johnson, Heather Stalberg and her patient family members.

Canadian Cataloguing in Publication
Mastin, Colleayn, O. (Colleayn Olive),
North American ocean creatures

(Grasshopper series; 3)
Includes index.
ISBN 1-895910-25-0.

1. Marine fauna—North American—Juvenile literature. I. Sovak, Jan, 1953– II. Title. III. Series: Mastin, Colleayn O. (Colleayn Olive), Grasshopper series; 3.
QL122.2.M385 1997   j591.77'097   C7-910362-2

Printed in Canada

Index	Page
Dolphin	20
Dogfish	9
Electric Ray	17
Flying Fish	31
Goosefish	4
Great White Shark	18
Hagfish	27
Octopus	7
Orca (or Killer Whale)	25
Salmon	14
Sea Anemone	22
Sea Horse	12
Sturgeon	28